This Bloomsbury book

belongs to

....

For Jacobo, Paloma, Segismon, Julia and little Pepe

First published in Great Britain in 2008 by Bloomsbury Publishing Plc
36 Soho Square, London, W1D 3QY

Text & illustrations copyright © Joseph Theobald 2008
The moral right of the author / illustrator has been asserted

A CIP catalogue record of this book is available from the British Library

ISBN 978 0 7475 9486 4

Printed in China by South China Printing Company

1 3 5 7 9 10 8 6 4 2

All papers used by Bloomsbury Publishing are natural, recyclable products made from
wood grown in well-managed forests. The manufacturing processes conform to the
environmental regulations of the country of origin

Marvin Gets MAD!

Joseph Theobald

BLOOMSBURY
CHILDREN'S
BOOKS

One perfect morning Marvin and Molly found a
tree full of big, juicy apples.

There was one apple that Marvin really
wanted but no matter how high he jumped,
he couldn't quite reach it.

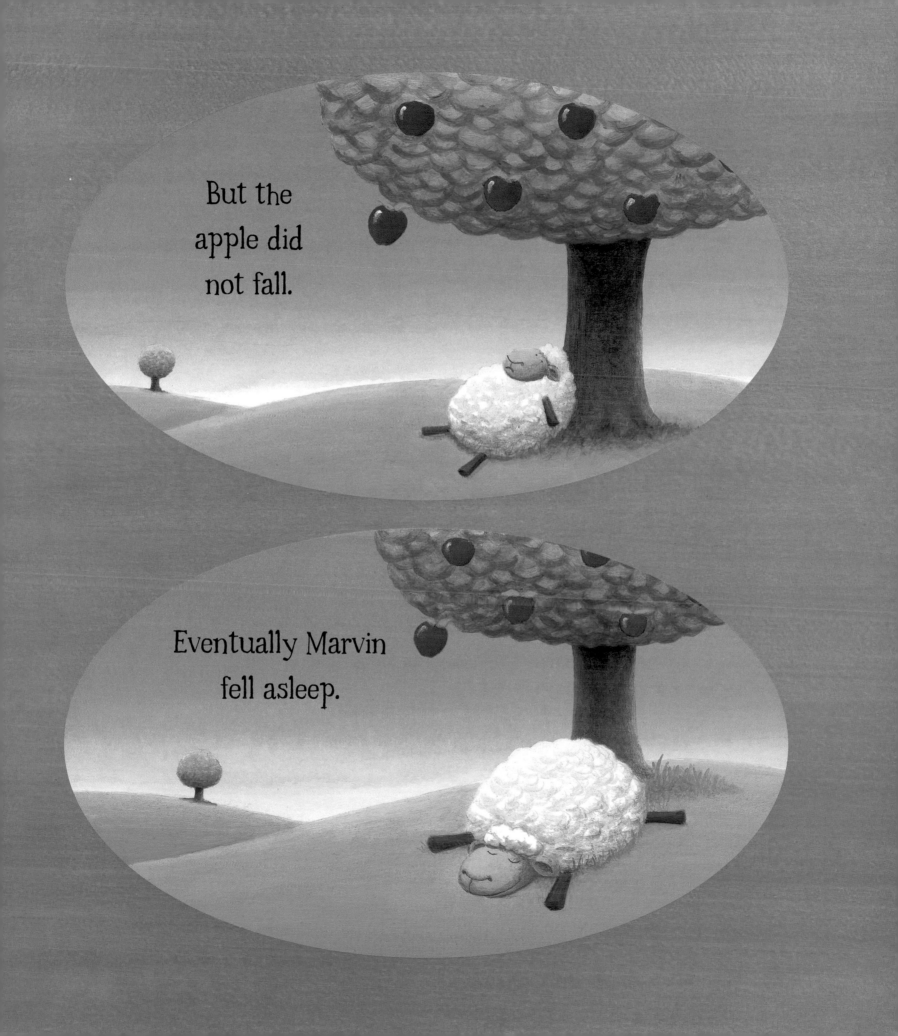

But the apple did not fall.

Eventually Marvin fell asleep.

When Marvin woke up, the apple was gone.
Molly was eating it!

"I wanted that apple!" shouted Marvin.
"Sorry," said Molly. "I didn't know."

Marvin was not happy.

"Don't get mad with me," said Molly.
"There are lots more apples in the tree."

"I WANTED THAT APPLE!" shouted Marvin.

"AND YOU'VE EATEN IT!!"

Marvin was so mad ... he grew
MAD teeth, MAD horns,
MAD feet, and a MAD tail.

"I WANT

MY APPLE!!"

"Calm down," said Molly.

"NO!" shouted Marvin, and he stamped on the flowers,

he knocked over the chicken shed,

he frightened the ducks,

and bit a cow's tail.

Marvin didn't know **what** he wanted any more.
He stamped his big mad feet and let out a big mad ...

As Marvin stamped harder and harder,
the ground began to rumble underneath him . . .
And suddenly . . .

CRACK

The ground opened up and
swallowed him whole.

Marvin fell deeper and
deeper and
landed with a thud, all
alone in the dark.

"BAAAA!" shouted Marvin, but no one could hear him.

He tried to break the wall, but that only hurt his head.

Marvin was all alone.

He closed his eyes and remembered
the perfect day in the meadow.
I wish Molly was here, he thought.
Gradually Marvin felt less mad.

When Marvin opened his eyes, there was Molly!
"I'm sorry I was so angry," said Marvin.
"That's OK," said Molly. "I came to find you.
I thought you might be lost. And look, I've found
another big, juicy apple. It's for you!"

"Thank you!" said Marvin.
And Molly showed Marvin the way
back up to the meadow.

Everything was perfect again.
But Marvin didn't want an apple any more . . .
He wanted a pear!

But no matter how high he jumped,
he couldn't quite reach it.